To **Emily**

For being good.
MERRY CHRISTMAS!

From

It was a crisp Christmas Eve
and Santa and his reindeers
were busy delivering presents to
all the good boys and girls.

Santa's sleigh zoomed over houses, twisting
and turning silently through the snowy night sky.
Santa squeezed down and up and up and down
chimneys, carefully and quietly delivering
lots of presents.

All was going to plan until he reached the second to last house on his list.

Suddenly, Santa realised one of the presents was missing!

The reindeer looked in Santa's sack, they searched everywhere but the present was nowhere to be found! "Oh no!" exclaimed Santa. "It must have fallen off the sleigh!"

5

Santa wondered what to do.
He had no time to look for the present
but he didn't want to disappoint anyone
on his Christmas list.

Then
Santa had a
FANTASTIC
idea!

Naughty & Nice
LIST

He looked at his delivery map to see where they were.
Then he checked his list to see who had been naughty or nic

At the very
top of the list was Emily.
So Santa and Blitzen (the smallest of
all the reindeer) squeezed
down the chimney...

Emily's
House

her

into

quietly

crept

...and

bedroom.

Emily yawned,
stretched and rubbed
her eyes. She thought she
was still **dreaming** until Blitzen licked her
face with his long, wet, pink tongue - YUCK!

8

"I need your help!" boomed Santa. He explained that a present had fallen off the sleigh and Santa wanted **Emily** to go with Blitzen to find it.

Emily of course was VERY happy to help.

9

It was cold and snowy outside so Emily put on her warmest hat and favourite stripy scarf.

Emily and Blitzen looked through Santa's telescope.

They looked down past the houses and through the trees, trying to find the lost present.

Suddenly they spotted it, sitting on top of a pile of snow at the bottom of a big hill.

10

She jumped on Blitzen's back and gave him a friendly pat and little tickle behind his fluffy ears.
Then with a gentle nudge they flew high into the starry night sky.

Up and up they soared

and higher

higher

until Blitzen did a
loop the loop,
a flip and a flop
and landed with a bop
next to the pile of snow...

but the present had gone

Emily and Blitzen looked around but couldn't see the present anywhere!

All of a sudden Blitzen's wet nose began to twitch and itch and wibble and wobble. What had he found?

Emily saw a bright orange carrot sticking out of the snow. "Who likes carrots?" she wondered. Perhaps this was a clue to where the present had gone.

Then they saw a tiny white and grey bunny rabbit

"Hello Mrs Rabbit, we're **looking** for a missing gift which fell from Santa's sleigh. Have you seen **anything**?"

The bunny **twitched** her nose, rubbed her ears and **pointed** a fluffy white paw at a line of acorns.

"Who likes acorns?"
wondered Emily.

Then looking down they noticed a
bouncy red squirrel staring back at them.
They followed him, picking up the acorns one by one,
not knowing who or what would be at the end of the trail.

As they picked up the final acorn,
they noticed a nose-less,
button-less, very sad snowman
right in front of them.

His carrot nose had fallen
off and his acorn
buttons had been
lost but there,
poking out from
under his black hat,
was a shiny
Christmas present!

Hurray, they had found the present... but why did the snowman have it?

The sad snowman explained that every year he felt forgotten as he never received a present. When he found this one he was so happy. However, now he knew it belonged to someone else, he wanted to give it back.

Feeling sorry for the snowman,
Emily decided to help.
She placed the half-eaten **carrot**
on the snowman's face for his nose
and the **acorn** buttons on his body –
but the snowman still looked sad.

Then **Emily**
had a brilliant idea!

She undid her **favourite woolly** scarf and tied it around the surprised snowman.

Then she replaced the snowman's old black hat with her warm knitted one.

The snowman was so happy! At last he had his very OWN Christmas present!

Emily and Blitzen flew as fast as they could to get the missing present back in time for Christmas morning.

Back at home Emily gave Blitzen a big hug, then watched as her new friend flew up into the sky and home to Santa.

Emily placed the gift under the tree with a huge sigh of relief!

20

When Emily woke up on Christmas morning, she wondered if it had all been a dream. Then she looked out of her window...

...and there in the distance was the happy snowman waving at her and he was still wearing his lovely Christmas present.

The end

21